Charlie the Caterpillar

Andy Gutman

First published by Dog Ear Publishing
4011 Vincennes Rd
Indianapolis, IN 46268
www.dogearpublishing.net

ISBN: 978-1-4575-6073-6

This book is printed on acid-free paper.

This book is a work of fiction. Places, events, and situations in this book are purely fictional and any resemblance to actual persons, living or dead, is coincidental.

Printed in the United States of America

Oh, this is the story of a cute caterpillar
Looking in the mirror and wishing he was bigger.
Doesn't know it now, but he is a winner
Everybody else can see.

This is the story of a cute caterpillar
Feeling like he's small but he wants to be bigger.
But he's got it wrong because nobody ever
Told him that he was unique.

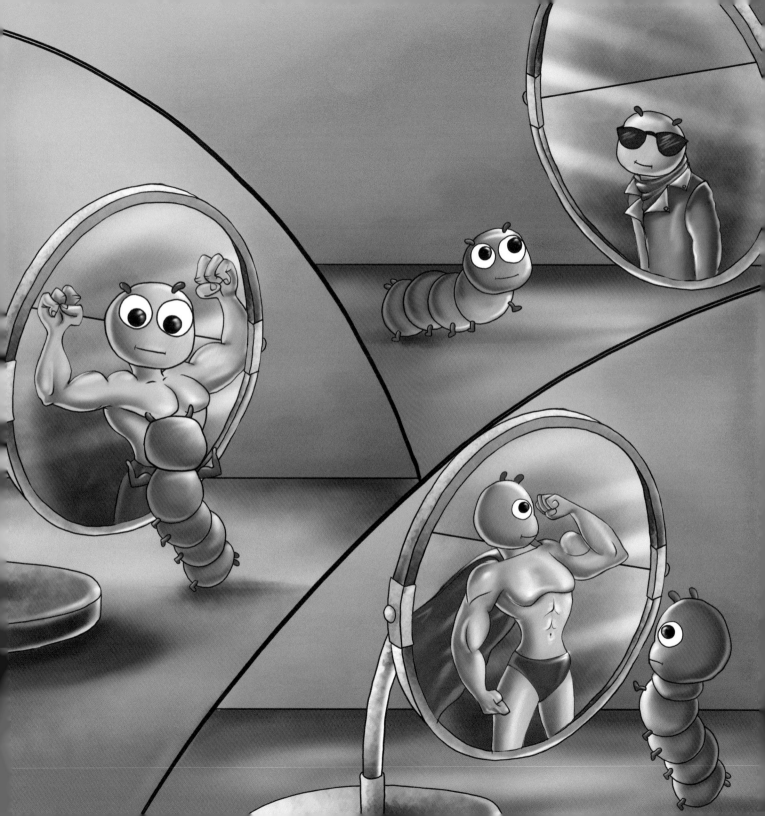

Charlie,
He is kind to all he meets,
Super cute and super sweet.

He's pretty quick on his caterpillar feet.
No one would ever call him weak!
Yet he can't help but compete,
Feeling that he's incomplete.

Charlie, Charlie,
Don't despair.
It doesn't matter what suit you wear.
Everybody deserves a chance—
It doesn't matter what suit they wear.

Now he's spinning around, and he made a cocoon.
Finally settles in to this nice little room.
Hoping at the end all the colors will bloom
And he'll be a masterpiece.

Charlie,
You can try on different wings,
Pretty outfits, gorgeous things,
Even ones fit for a king ...

You're starting
To become what you had dreamed,
In time you're going to see
All that matters is what's beneath.

Oh, now he's coming out of the cocoon as he takes to the sky,
Zipping all around as a bright butterfly.
Looking at the ground, and he thinks in his mind,
Why am I not satisfied?

Oh, Charlie,
You just have to be yourself:
Only you and no one else.
If they don't like you, then, oh well.

Charlie,
It doesn't matter what you've got—
Neon stripes or polka dots—
Raise your head and show them off!

Charlie, Charlie,
Don't despair!
It doesn't matter what suit you wear.
Everybody deserves a chance—
it doesn't matter what suit they wear.

The end

CPSIA information can be obtained at www.ICGtesting.com
Printed in the USA
LVIW01n1826141217
559762LV00002B/2

9781457560736